ZANDER'S FRIENDSHIP JOURNEY

DOROTHY E. HARDIN

"*In this thoughtful debut children's book by a veteran educator, a first-grader with difficulty relating to others embarks on a "friendship journey" and socially blossoms with help from caring adults.*"

Kirkus Indie Review

For Luke, my inspiration, and Mr. Wayne, my husband and editor

Before writing children's fiction, Dorothy E. Hardin was an award-winning teacher and principal and university college of education lecturer/supervisor. Having written many nationally published articles and op-ed pieces, she now is a consultant and writing coach.

Her little friends call her Miss Dottie. To them, she is a fun storyteller. *Zander's Friendship Journey* evolved from a series of "social stories," written for children struggling with peer relationships.

Miss Dottie's online contacts include:
> Facebook – Writer's Page (Dorothy E. Hardin - Author)
> Gmail (dcehardin44@gmail.com)
> Twitter (Dorothy E. Hardin @DottieHardin)

Contents

Chapter 1:

Zander Meets His New Teachers

Once upon a time, there was a boy named Zander. He was six years old. Zander stayed with his grandmother, Nana.

Nana homeschooled Zander, using books, puzzles, games, and a computer. She made learning fun.

One day, Zander's mommy and daddy decided he should attend their neighborhood school. They wanted Zander to learn new things and be with other children at Spring Creek Elementary School. It was a school with nice teachers and friendly boys and girls.

As the days passed, Zander became excited about attending elementary school. Zander looked forward to meeting his teachers, Mrs. Perez and Miss Rivers, and the children in his class. He felt almost ready for his school adventure.

On the first day of school, Zander and Nana walked slowly down the hallway toward the Terrific Tadpoles Grades 1-2 Classroom.

Mrs. Perez and Miss Rivers stood in the doorway, greeting the children. "Hello, Kippy! Hi, Yukako! Hello, Emmy Lee! Hi, Zander!"

After ten days of school, Zander told Miss Joy, a family friend, "Sometimes my teachers seem unhappy with me."

"How do you know they are unhappy?" Miss Joy asked.

"Their mouths look frowny and sad," Zander answered quietly.

Miss Joy asked, "Do you know why they are sad?"

Zander sighed. "Not exactly," he said.

Zander began to notice that even Nana seemed unhappy. He did not know that his teachers had spoken to Nana about him.

Zander knew he needed help from Miss Joy. "I know how to make your teachers happy, Zander," said Miss Joy. "Do you say 'hi' and give your teachers a big smile when you see them in the morning?"

"No," said Zander.

"OK, Zander. Try saying hello to Mrs. Perez and Miss Rivers when you first see them. Then, give them a big smile. They will like your friendly greeting."

"No!" Zander said. "I don't want to do that."

Miss Joy spoke softly. "Zander, do you like me to smile at you?" she asked. Zander nodded.

"Do you like me to say nice things to you when we are playing together?" Miss Joy asked.

"Yes," said Zander.

"Think about how happy your teachers might feel when you smile and say 'hi' to them.

"Look at your teacher's eyes with your eyes," Miss Joy added. "Try that when Mrs. Perez or Miss Rivers talks to you directly. Keep your eyes locked on their eyes. It's called eye contact."

Miss Joy explained that Zander was on a friendship journey at Spring Creek Elementary School.

She said that the first part of his journey would involve making eye contact, saying "hi," and smiling.

Zander remembered that Mrs. Perez and Miss Rivers told him many times each day, "One! Two! Three! Look at me!"

Zander wanted to make his teachers happy. He better understood the need to look at Mrs. Perez and Miss Rivers when they spoke to him.

Miss Joy locked her eyes on Zander's eyes and gave him a big smile. "Are you ready to do some greeting, smiling, and eyeball-locking next week at school?" she asked.

"You are so funny, Miss Joy!" Zander laughed, locking his eyes on hers.

Zander hoped that saying "hello" or "hi" would make his teachers happy and open the door to making new friends.

Zander practiced saying "hello" when Poppy, his grandfather, came home from work. He practiced smiling and saying "hello" to Miss Joy on her visits. He practiced looking into Nana's eyes when she asked him for help.

Zander decided that his next practice was going to be real at Spring Creek Elementary School.

On Tuesday, Zander greeted Mrs. Perez and Miss Rivers at the classroom door. "Hello!" Zander said.

Looking up, Zander realized how difficult it was to eyeball both teachers and smile at the same time. Although Zander's smile was crooked and wobbly, it was his best smile.

Spring Creek Elementary School

Spring Creek
Elementary School

Miss Rivers smiled and said, "Zander, it's so nice to see you." Mrs. Perez added, "You have made us feel so happy this morning."

"Yay, me!" Zander thought.

Then, Zander had a new idea. He would walk over to the brown-haired girl, Emmy Lee.

Looking into her eyes, he would bravely smile and say, "Hi, Emmy Lee!" Zander hoped this special greeting would lead to the next part of his friendship journey.

Chapter 2:

Zander Shares a Hamburger Book

Zander enjoyed being in Spring Creek Elementary School and his Terrific Tadpoles classroom every day.

On a chilly Wednesday, Mrs. Perez and Miss Rivers, his teachers, stood in the doorway, smiling. They greeted their children, "Good morning, Terrific Tadpoles! Hello, Kyle! Hi, Yukako! Hi, Louis! Hello, Zander!"

Zander said, "Hi, Mrs. Perez! Miss Rivers! It's nice to see you!" Zander knew that smiling and saying something positive made his teachers smile, too. Zander felt ready to begin his day.

Zander wondered where Emmy Lee was. He wanted to say "hi" to her. As Zander thought about Emmy Lee, she walked into the room. Miss Rivers pointed to the empty seat next to Zander. Emmy Lee smiled. Zander felt that his friendship journey was going very well.

Often, Miss Joy, Zander's friend, reminded him that the friendship journey could be tricky. Zander knew he had to focus on the feelings of others. This was very hard since Zander didn't always understand his own feelings.

Then, Mrs. Perez said loudly, "Eyes on me, please!" She was ready to give directions. "As you know, Wednesday is our book day. Today, we are going to do something new with books! Are you ready to do something new?"

"Yes!" the children yelled. For Zander, the word *"new"* could mean a fun adventure or a scary experience. His "yes" was not as enthusiastic as Emmy Lee's.

Mrs. Perez asked the children to share a book with their seat partners. Emmy Lee ran to the bookshelf for her favorite book. She placed HORRIBLE HAMBURGERS AND FRIZZY FRIES, OH MY! in front of Zander.

Although it was one of his favorites, too, Zander did not understand why he had to share. Mrs. Perez asked if he would "please" share the book with Emmy Lee.

"No," Zander said softly. "I don't want to do that."

Emmy Lee wanted to share this favorite book with her friend, Zander. Now, he seemed angry with her.

Mrs. Perez gently said, "Zander, look at Emmy Lee's unhappy face. Why won't you share HORRIBLE HAMBURGERS AND FRIZZY FRIES, OH MY! with her? Emmy Lee would enjoy that. I bet it would be fun for you, too."

As Zander thought about Emmy Lee's unhappy face, he made a choice. Zander decided to share the book with Emmy Lee.

Zander trusted Mrs. Perez. She was trying to help him understand sharing. Zander was learning that sometimes it is important to share, even when he may not want to.

As Zander began to share HORRIBLE HAMBURGERS AND FRIZZY FRIES, OH MY!, Emmy Lee moved closer to him. Zander smiled inside. Turning the pages, Zander and Emmy Lee smiled and laughed at the funny hamburger pictures.

As Zander read the sentences and gave her a nod, Emmy Lee would say, "Oh My!" at just the right time.

Mrs. Perez and Miss Rivers were pleased that both children were sharing and looking so happy.

Emmy Lee said, "Zander, you are a great reader!" Looking into her eyes, Zander smiled and said, "Thanks, Emmy Lee."

Zander felt proud of himself for sharing. He wondered what his next adventure would be at Spring Creek Elementary School. Although there might be surprises or difficulties ahead, Zander hoped that his friendship journey would have a happy ending.

Chapter 3:

Zander Takes a Tadpole Turn

Each week, Zander saw his teachers greeting the children as they entered the Terrific Tadpoles Grades 1-2 Classroom. "Hello, Kippy! Hello, Zander!"

With a large smile, Zander said, "Hi, Mrs. Perez! Hi, Miss Rivers!" If he saw Emmy Lee across the room, he'd wave to her, too. "Hi, Emmy Lee!"

On Wednesday during a new book-sharing activity, Mrs. Perez said, "Tadpoles, I want you to share another book with a friend at your table." Zander was not sure if he should choose the book or if Emmy Lee would choose again.

Zander asked Emmy Lee if she would like to read a book with numbers in it. Shaking her head from side to side, Emmy Lee said, "No! I don't like numbers."

Zander was surprised since he loved to count and look at numbers. Zander already had learned to count from 1 to 1000 on Nana's computer.

When Emmy Lee brought BUMBLE BEE, BUMBLE BEE, WHY DO YOU BUZZ? from the bookshelf, it did not make Zander happy. Before they became friends, he might have chosen to sit alone or walk away. Now, Zander worried about how Emmy Lee might feel.

Then, Zander thought of TEN TERRIFIC TADPOLES. It was a binder book that Miss Rivers had written for her "tadpoles." Since only ten tadpoles were in the book, Zander hoped that would be OK with Emmy Lee.

Zander brought the binder book to the table. Emmy Lee frowned when Zander read the title, TEN TERRIFIC TADPOLES.

"I don't want to read TEN TERRIFIC TADPOLES!" Emmy Lee snapped.

Miss Rivers saw that Zander and Emmy Lee were having a problem. Miss Rivers said kindly, "Emmy Lee, this is a fun book to read. I enjoyed writing it for all of my tadpoles."

Then, Miss Rivers said firmly, "Emmy Lee, last time, you picked out HORRIBLE HAMBURGERS AND FRIZZY FRIES, OH MY!. This time, it is Zander's turn to select a book."

Miss Rivers said calmly, "Emmy Lee, look at me, please. You need to allow Zander to take his turn. I'm sure you will have fun reading his book."

Opening the first page of the binder book, Zander began:

Ten terrific tadpoles leaping in the creek,
One tad bumped his head and screamed a big "EEK!"
Their teacher called the doctor and his voice did shriek,
"Stop those tadpoles leaping in the creek!"

Emmy Lee uncrossed her arms. She leaned toward Zander as he read the second verse:

Nine terrific tadpoles leaping in the creek,
One tad scraped his tail and started to freak.
Their teacher called the doctor and his voice did shriek,
"Stop those tadpoles leaping in the creek!"

Emmy Lee smiled when Zander held up nine fingers to show the number of tadpoles. Miss Rivers and Mrs. Perez smiled, as Zander continued to read.

Before Zander began the last verse, Emmy Lee spoke in a squeaky voice. "I'm a terrific tadpole, too!"

Both children giggled.

Zander recited the final lines of the rhyme from memory:

One terrific tadpole leaping in the creek,
This tad hit a rock and looked quite weak.
Their teacher called the doctor and his voice did shriek,
"Stop those tadpoles leaping in the creek!"

Later that afternoon, Zander told his parents, grandparents, and Miss Joy about his day in school. His teachers and Emmy Lee had helped him learn about taking turns. His family and Miss Joy were proud of him.

Zander was proud and happy, too. He felt prepared for another adventure on his friendship journey at Spring Creek Elementary School.

Chapter 4:

Zander Makes a New Friend

Zander looked forward to saying "hi" to his teachers, as he entered the Terrific Tadpoles Grades 1-2 Classroom.

"Hello, Zander!" said Mrs. Perez.

"Hi, Mrs. Perez!" Zander replied.

"How are you today?" asked Miss Rivers.

Zander smiled, "I'm fine, Miss Rivers." And in fact, he did feel very fine.

Today, Zander thought he might do an activity with one of the boys in the classroom. Would it be Kyle? Would it be Kippy?

Also, Zander thought it would be nice to have one more friend in Spring Creek Elementary School. Zander felt eager about the next part of his friendship journey.

Ready to give directions, Mrs. Perez asked the children for their attention. "Eyes on me, please! That means you, Nikki. And you, Emmy Lee."

Mrs. Perez said, "It's time for us to color pictures of farm animals. Please choose a new partner, now."

Zander turned to Miss Rivers, "If it's OK, I would like to color with Kippy." Kippy nodded and moved next to Zander.

Zander wondered what animals they would color and how they would choose the colors. Suddenly, Kippy asked, "What's your favorite ice cream?"

Zander stared at him. Kippy asked again in a louder voice. He thought Zander might not have heard his question. Zander finally replied, "Strawberry." Zander was not interested in talking about ice cream. He was interested in coloring.

Mrs. Perez walked over to the boys, sensing that things were not going smoothly. Kippy blurted, "Mrs. Perez, I asked Zander about his favorite ice cream, but he didn't ask me about mine."

"Zander, don't you want to have a conversation with Kippy?" asked Mrs. Perez.

"I thought we were coloring," Zander replied. "What's a conversation?"

Mrs. Perez explained. "A conversation is something that people enjoy. We share our thoughts, feelings, likes, and dislikes. Conversations help build friendships. Kippy wants to be your friend. He was trying to figure out what you like. That's why Kippy was asking you about your favorite ice cream."

Zander thought about conversation. It sounded very hard to do. "Mrs. Perez," he said. "I don't know if I can color and have a conversation at the same time."

Mrs. Perez smiled. "Of course you can, Zander. You can do anything you put your mind to."

Zander saw that Kippy was frowning. Wanting to make things better, Zander asked a question: "Kippy, do you like strawberry ice cream?"

Kippy replied slowly, "I like it, but my very favorite ice cream is chocolate."

Before giving them the picture to color, Mrs. Perez asked, "What is your favorite farm animal?"

Immediately, the boys said, "Cows!" Zander and Kippy laughed.

"Well, boys, this is your lucky day! Here's a picture with four cows for you to color!" Zander and Kippy were very happy. It was their lucky day.

They colored the four cows milk-chocolate brown.
Kippy said, "Maybe we should color the sky pink, like strawberry ice cream." Zander agreed that pink would be a perfect color for the sky.

"What color should we make the fence?"
Zander asked. "Maybe we should choose white.
We already used brown on the cows." Kippy said,
"Or it could be red. That's one of my favorite colors."

"A red fence?" Zander asked. "You are so silly, Kippy." The boys laughed together.

"Do you like to drink milk, Zander?" Kippy asked.

"Nope! I like to drink water." Then, Zander thought of something else he enjoyed, "What about snow angels? I love to make them in my backyard."

"Really? I love making snow angels, too," said Kippy, as Zander reached for a red crayon.

Zander and Kippy's completed picture had brown cows standing behind a red fence in a green pasture. The sky was strawberry pink with white clouds and a purple sun.

The boys laughed and had a real conversation –
a very fine conversation between two new friends.

Finally, Zander understood his friendship journey.
It was just beginning, and he was not alone.

Made in the USA
Lexington, KY
18 December 2014